# Swallowed

| Swallowed

X.
*Constantine*

ISBN #: 9798860020740

# | author's note

This story is fiction. All characters written in this story are eighteen years or older.

| 1

A wind whipped restlessly against the windowpane, the sound of water striking the ground outside carrying a heavy scent of the rainfall as Melody Frost lay upon her bed, eyes gazing upon the ceiling fan as it spun in the dim light of her bedroom. She heard the sound of her music playing lightly in the darkness of the closet, the echo of Kelly Rowland belting out the tune "Stole". In the hallway, she heard the sound of voices, the noise of her mother talking on the phone, and the tone of her voice. Almost ashamed to hear it, Melody turned on her side, facing away from the noise, and continued to hear the noise of the song as it filtered through the chamber she was in, the noise of it a restless bellow of emotion that filtered out how she felt.

Her mother could be heard talking calmly, yet with concern in her voice. The sound of they way she felt portrayed the understanding that Melody was in trouble. She knew she had done something wrong. Hence the detention she had received the remainder of the day in class. Having ended up in the principle's office after kicking a girl who she had argued with in the hallway at her locker. Right between the legs.

Melody shifted, her legs themselves moving as what was between them became suddenly stiff. Swollen. She felt it herself. The knowledge of what she had soon learned as visiting the nurse's office afterward, the girl, a known goth, who, held back as she had been herself a few years, was witness to having been given the same parts as she, when born.

Squeezing her eyes shut as she heard her mother slam the phone down, she heard the footsteps coming to her door and then the knob turned. There was no knock to be heard. Her mother knew she awake. The music was turned down as the noise of Panic at the Disco could be heard filling the void, growing quiet. The song "I Write Sins Not Tragedies" being lowered to a softer tone.

"What is it about you getting along with people that you don't seem to understand?" her mother stated without entering the conversation with a level of knowledge that she was given any choice to pause before letting her daughter speak. "That girl is upset as much as her mother seems to be. She told me to have you apologize."

Melody furrowed her brow, turning to look at her mother with a look of disdain. "I will, don't worry," she said. Turning over on her side, she closed her eyes, feeling embarrassed. "As soon as the weekend is over. On Monday I'll walk right up to her and tell her 'I'm so sorry I kicked you in the woman's part of your actual *manhood.*'"

"Young lady you will apologize. *Today.*"

"How is that?"

"She's coming over. To see you herself."

Melody blanched, turning over to sit on the edge of the bed, and stare. Her eyes widened. "Here? Her mother is coming?"

"No," her mother said. "She is."

"Here?"

"Yes. Today. I will be leaving as soon as she is here, I need to go and set a good example for you by letting the principle know myself that you *will* be making up for what you did today." She walked to the door and as she was closing it, she said, "You *are* going to apologize. Whether you like it or not."

The door shut loudly, and Melody slumped back on the bed, her legs still on the edge, feet touching the floor. She groaned, grabbing her pillow and screaming into it until she felt the breath in her chest was gone and taking a deep breath, groaned again before standing up and turning up the song, went to sit down on the edge of her bed and placing her face in her hands, prepared herself to be greeted by the one person she last expected to see, yet again, on the last day of the week.

It was going to be a long weekend.

| 2

Melody had heard the sound of her mother leaving the driveway almost five minutes after shutting her bedroom door. Her breath caught in her chest as she listened to the song she had been listening to ending. It was followed by the next tune. A song by The Used.

"Let it Bleed."

*Let it bleed . . . watch the fire fill your lungs.*

A little bit by the singer whose name was Bert McCracken, a high school dropout become music icon, filled her room.

*You feel like dying, you might wanna* SIIIIINNG!

Breathing a sigh of aggravation, she held her breath as she took a moment to close her eyes and seeing her face in the darkness beyond the image of what happened, she found her emotions running platonic to the point of making her feel sick and irritated.

She wanted to understand why she had done what she did. The knowledge that she knew why she was where she had become now as a sudden struggle because she knew that what she had done was wrong and she should never have made the issue public. The principle hadn't seen it. The girls in the hallway had seen it and she knew that her own friends had not even given a damn. She knew the girl was struggling the way she cried out, gripping her loin area where she screamed in pain. A sudden gasp, a knowledge in understanding that after pushing Melody against the locker had made her feel more than unwelcome.

The song ended, followed by "All that I've Got."

*I'm far from lonely, and it's all that I've got . . . I guess . . . I scrubbed so hard . . . So deep that I didn't even . . . scream—*

Knock, *knock.*

"*Fuck* me," Melody muttered, following the lyrics on the track as she sat up, walking to the stereo and turning the song down, turned her slender fingers into a fist as she reached for the knob with hesitation and feeling the cool knob between her fingers, turned the handle, greeting the person who stood on the other side.

She was dressed in a thin white tee shirt ripped at the neckline to reveal a scar on her shoulder. There was a slight gap at the space below her midriff that revealed her toned stomach and below the baggy sweats shrouded by the hoodie that covered her lower half, oversized. The shoes she wore covered bare feet within and as the dark brooding eyes met her stare looking her over, Melody looked back, seeing the gaze of malcontent and understanding how the two of them felt separated by the judgment in the incident of both their day.

"Hey, Luna," Melody said.

The other girl stared back, her sharp Asian features beautiful, but with a slight hint of leaked mascara and her gaze which had recently built upon the effect of the new knowledge between them.

"Hey," Luna said. She looked around the room, surveying her former enemy and her once dormant kingdom, surrendering a look at the bed and gesturing to the stereo at a lower tone of music that continued to play. "You like The Used?"

Melody curled her lip distastefully. "I feel Used." She saw the look of concern in the young woman's eyes. Sighing she gestured to the bed. "You want to come in, or what?"

Luna shrugged. Melody stepped aside and then as she walked inside, Melody shut the door, resting her head against the wood. Unfurling her fingers from the knob, she pressed her back against it and folding her arms, looked at Luna who had taking a seat on the floor, and as she glimpsed her stature of gazing up at her, she noticed the slight bit of flame in her gaze. A sort of almost tipsy flower of ecstasy within.

"Your mom told me," she stated, "you have . . . what I have too. I should have given you a chance. To understand we're not that different."

Melody shook her head, throwing up her hands at her sides. "You're point is?"

Folding her hands over her lap, there was a slight moment where the other person in the room lowered her head, her raven and red bangs falling across her face in shadow. On the stereo the song "Yesterday's Feelings" filled the room with the echo of Bert McCracken's somber tones.

Melody sighed. "I'm sorry. I shouldn't have been so rude myself."

A moment passed in silence between them. As the lull was broken two words were uttered. It was Luna.

"Can I see it?"

| 3

Melody had heard the words. She had felt the sudden question within her own mind, wondering if she felt how inquired she had, a sudden method in the relationship between, somehow *actually* platonic.

But *was* it *still*?

*Real?* Melody asked herself this, biting her lip. She saw the gaze coming as Luna razored a look at her in question. She asked her again.

"Can I see it? If you show me, I will show you mine." A slight smile played across the young woman's lips. "We can, you know . . . *compare*." Her tone manipulated seductive, though the feeling that Melody had was uncertain. Luna's eyes still somehow blazed brown, though within, something odd shown. A sort of almost strange, predator like stare.

She herself was leaving it to the unknown. Her mother had asked her to connect, to share the feeling between them as one, and to understand that she had done wrong in the first place. It was wonder why she had committed to believe this was going to happen at all. As she sighed, glancing behind her, to the closed door and the hallway beyond, she found herself questioning the possibility that her mother was going to arrive, show up and within the moment she found herself believing she could be found almost in between the ecstasy of Luna's stare and her ... mouth ...

Melody closed her eyes, biting her lip as she suddenly swelled, her legs squeezing together as if to bite back the erection spreading out in her pants. Pressing against the denim.

Then, as she stood, entranced by the wanton sensation between her legs, a moment of explosive feeling that became numb, almost like a drug, filled her, and she was stuck, imagining the feeling of lips wrapped around her, the sudden warmth of a tongue resting against her groin and licking her member, swallowing her shaft down, into the depths of an unknown impressive throat.

*I'm so far gone . . . do you wanna take me on?*

Bert McCracken started to sing "*Lunacy Fringe*". An almost tipsy echo filled her as her eyes opened. She saw Luna standing. She hadn't heard her rise from the floor. It was then that she saw her reaching for the spot between her legs.

A bulge had begun to rise. A thickness within that pulsed. Growing to a rising warmth within.

Melody felt her mouth begin to water in anticipation of the newest pleasure.

# | 4

*Would you be my little .... Would you be my thousand cuts?*

"I'm a Fake" by The Used.

Entranced by emotions she felt she couldn't control. The swelling of desire that she wanted so long; the distance of the last time almost seemed to make her feel wet, and Melody saw herself walking over, gazing at her once known enemy and seeing a flirting desire. She saw the young woman before her, the intense burn of her brazen brown eyes below dark Asian brows. Furrowing her gaze, she reached down and felt the hand reaching for hers. Her tongue traced the lips of her own mouth, and Luna smiled, pressing her own mouth against Melody's.

Melody gasped, feeling the tension between them, a sudden emotional tension and desire that was so expressive, so wanton and intense she almost felt the graze of the second member, the other one behind cotton and cloth, rubbing against her own.

# | 5

A tingling sensation, trickling down the back of her spine. She could feel the pressure of tongue against her own, the fingers reaching out, grasping her lap, rubbing slowly between her legs, tensing up the rush of adrenaline to become more than an imaginative ploy. More than imaginary. More than platonic.

Realistic.

Erotic.

*Want-*

She looked at the face in her eyes, hearing a fresh guitar, electric, a solo, like almost near, but in her head. The sound of a heavy voice, almost gluing itself.

*Some of them want to be .... I want to use you, and ....* Inside *you.*

Marilyn Manson sang "Sweet Dreams are Made of This".

Luna's hands grasped her shaft, stroking it, inside her fly, grasping the member as it pulsated, almost missing to her likeness of connection between them, the bodies of them intertwined almost like glue, the feeling of sensation in the moment such a gratified explosion waiting to happen.

"My mom will be—*home* soon," Melody stammered. Luna placed a hand, almost firmly, but with tender care, over her mouth, and she closed her eyes, facing the dawn of what was to be a sudden ripple of time, growing longer between them. The tensions were high.

We're dead . . . we *know* ... who we-

"Fu*ck*," Melody hissed, feeling the sudden tickle of a warmth rubbing itself against her glands, noticing the heat beyond, almost stunning her as she looked at her lower half, down below where her thighs rested, now exposed, seeing the spot of her pubic region and the shaft, protruding, having been extracted and exposed. The lips tickled her region of lap, and she found her eyes staring, entranced as the ones that blazed gazed back, almost emotional, but somehow emotionless ...

Then, it dawned, as the lips parted, the strength of a sucking that Melody never thought she experienced, as if her soul was leaving and the music seemed almost distant.

*To make us feel . . . cops and . . . hate today. No love for tomorrow ...*

In the *dope*—

"Damn me," Melody felt as if her shaft was being inhaled. An intense emotion of feeling the reality in orgasmic question of suddenly knowing she could be inhaled as such, yet she was not close. "How are you-?"

*Shhhh ...*

The voice hushed her as her shaft seemed to disappear, growing closed within the membrane of a mouth unsavory, unwilling to know how much she was teased by its heat within. She gasped, feeling the rhetoric question dissipate into her head like the bad memory of yesterday.

*Swallowing* me?

The dick sat in the back of an enveloping warm throat, that seemed like a chasm in itself, the brazen eyes gazing up at her and she found her face twitching with ecstasy her gaze carrying the realism that was her fate to decide—

"I'm going *to . .* uh-huh*nn.*"

So close. So*oo* cl*ooo*se*e.*

Melody's thighs trembled.

# | 6

She jolted awake, sweating, the sudden explanation of orgasm dissipating as a thought traveled, faintly into the echo of a dark room she couldn't believe to be suddenly real. The imagination of what had just happened, so real, the dawn of what was to come to be unknown.

Melody blanched with her body drenched in sweat. She heard the song in the distant of her bedroom closet, the noise of the song . . .

*Now I know . . . I've got to ... get—*

*Away.*

*Tainted Love. Marilyn Manson.*

Beneath the covers, her shaft seemed to tremble, almost twitch. She felt the tenderness of a slim yet stiffened cock resting against satin and glanced at the clock, glowing green numerals in the dark. The casting image of what were the time stamps in the night hitting her retinas within her eyes: 3:28.

The witching hour.

# | 7

She stood in the shower stalls, gazing upon the dripping of water through strands of her hair, the locker room echoing with the laughter and cacophonies of young women gossiping. Such a noise that it drowned out the noise of a song in the back room. The lockers where other students were chatting, getting undressed and going to shower. Soon the place was filled with laughing, chuckles, and giggles.

I didn't know I believed the truth but..

You couldn't tell the way she was screaming?

The echo of a cry so longing to believe that she was just such a little who—!

"Hey!"

Hands grasped her shoulders, squeezing, turning her around to face dripping hair, blonde, and covering nipples turned pink from the heat of the shower. A taut stomach leading to slender legs and in between, freshly shaved pink, moist labia, puffy, as if having experienced the heat of sex.

"You are the one who kicked Luna in the sack, right?" the woman's name was Sam. She could be such a controlling person sometimes and Melody understood that.

Melody's nose twitched as she saw two other girls behind Sam, noticing the tension of the group. One was named Kenna, and she was also a blonde, more bosomed and sort of thicker in the breasts. The patch between her legs protruded with a swollen circumcised penis that swayed above balls that had remained full with some time. She watched the silver blue eyes gaze at her from still wet hair that had just showered. Next to her stood Jess, a standout but someone who was alone among them.

She was nervous, seeming to glance over her shoulder at the others, but remained wary of the fact that she was new to the group. Between her legs, a pink, erect, slim shaft stood stiff and tense like a flagpole against clean shaven skin and a pink pair of testicles. Her feet were as pale as her member, and her body was tense as well. She looked around, almost fearful.

Of somethin-?

"Ugh!" Melody felt the knee drive itself home, the explosion of sudden nerves creating an emotion of agony between her legs as her groin erupted in a searing pain of the notion to create the words—

You *deserved* IT

Crying out, the other girl stepped back in shock, as Sam took hold of Melody's scalp and yanking back on her hair, dragged her forward until the face of hers was pressed into her freshly cleaned groin.

"EAT IT *BITCH*! I SAAIID EAT THE CUNT!"

"Mphhmmhghh."

"Eat my pussy you sack *kicking slut*. Eat the carpet that owns you."

Around them, a chant had begun. An echo of silence mingled with the sharpness of the one who controlled everyone. A new dream of pleasure as she found herself growing closer to becoming erotic. The throbbing pain in Melody's lower half of her body had dulled to an ache and she found her body sagging with regret and commitment in giving Sam just what she wished.

Sharply, in the doubt of her mind, she knew she had been wrong. It had been a dream. She was only conscious of the knowledge that in retrospect, her aim to become understanding of what could have been imagined, may be real.

Could someone be there. To save her?

From this torment—

"I'm so fucking close . . . damn you're good at this. Fuck this feels amazing. Why are you *sooo* good at this . .. oh, God. I think I'm gonna cum. Don't you change your direction you little slu-!"

A scream erupted. An echo of cry from behind, among the crowd...

Behind her, Sam heard the howl of what she recognized as her friend Kenna. Her voice seemed to echo torment and pain, the muffled howl of a person in trouble.

The chanting had stopped.

# | 7

A muffled sound, screaming within the maw. Legs kicking wildly, madly in vain, the tone of a scream of sudden fear, knowing oneself to be in terrible fate of a grip that held it, and the life that which could end soon. Dark red eyes gazed upon the face, staring back as the jaw unhinged, swallowing more of the tormented bully, and the body seemed to disappear more, the cock and balls between the legs twitching as the warmth within seemed to almost tease the effect of the mouth itself intensifying an unknown, yet strange pleasure.

Sam gawked, feeling terror in her chest, looking only upon the head that was engulfing her friend, who was now slowly disappearing into the gullet of the monster. Her face twitched in fear as she found herself unable to move, a fear, almost candid she knew herself, to remain inside the adrenaline that had faded long before. Behind her, still on her knees, and in a blur of tears and the water pouring down upon her, Melody remained on the floor, broken, and with her nose bleeding from the stress of having witnessed the last punch from the girl who had flung her back, striking her in the nose. She looked up, a drop of blood dribbling from her left nostril and down her upper lip. She could hear, could almost feel the tension between her and the new bully in front of her. She could see the others in the locker room, some who had moved in panic, running from the scene. Among them, Jess stood, staring in fear as the legs of her unknown companion who had once welcomed her to the open arms a cult that was soon to be out of the picture, and herself was to witness the end of the one who had shaken her hand in the first place.

Seeing the feet still kicking madly, the face of Sam was filled with sudden panic and emotion, noticing how the dick had gone, only to somehow turn stiff, sliding the glands against the roof of the mouth and as it disappeared, the tongue of the beast wrapped around the base, encircling the stiffening cock and making it twitch. A hollow moan

within the throat seemed to echo and record
in the back of Sam's mind as Kenna
appeared in ecstasy as her feet, grown limp
and her legs following before, faded into the
black of the gullet as the monster gulped. She
saw her best friend's girth disappear into the
stomach content below, and suddenly, in a
motion of blurred image and a sort of smoke
that was like vapor, the beast changed,
growing limbs, like a bug's skeleton and a
mouth with pincers that sat on either side of
the toothed maw. The lips almost appeared
to turn grinning with the echo of an
exoskeleton and glowing yellow eyes with slits
for pupils turning red.

Sam screamed, stumbling back and
towards one of the closed stalls. She fell
backwards, crawling on her hands towards
the corner of it, out of the picture of the face
that filled Melody's frame of wet hair. She
wiped her nose, tasting blood and sat back
on the wall, almost in a daze as she heard
Sam utter a cry of panic and the young
women seemed to eye her more than witness
as the beast jerked forward and Sam's scream
was cut short. The monster stepped back on
thin legs, appearing to hold the engulfed

upper half of the bully, feet and ankles dangling below the maw as it turned its head to face Melody. She gasped as she saw the mouth open, the pincers on either side moving to push the limp calves down its gullet and swallowing, lifted its face towards the ceiling, giving out a harsh piercing screech.

Sam and Kenna were gone.

# | 8

Jess stumbled back, staring in fear at the face of the morphing monster. The one who had devoured her "friends" and newest group she had joined, only now she seemed to understand it was not okay, not right of her to have done what she did. She saw the face changing. Morphing into a sudden stare of amazed and wild tension that appeared like that of a maddening grin within the features of a predator ...

*Stalk*ing.

Melody watched in horror, seeing Jess dash towards the shower stalls to her left, and turning her face towards the monster as it moved forward, its flailing green tentacles appearing to morph, becoming claws, ever reaching, the feet pounded, bare and the nails, sharp and black, piercing tile, punctured the floor of the showers. Jess stumbled as the echo of a quake was followed by her knees buckling and she found herself scared, panicking as she turned to stare back at the leering mouth and the distant features beyond, the stomach she knew was waiting to digest her.

"No, no, wait I'm ... I'm sorry- I wasn't trying . . . please. PLEASE NO!"

Melody heard the panic in the young woman's voice. Amongst her former group, the girl had appeared uncertain, unaware of where she belonged. Now, ironically, she was going to join the throng of the three they had been.

In the belly of the beast that had devoured-

The other *two* ...

Stumbling towards the inner wall and the shower to her left, she found herself cut off as she moved towards the corner, pressing her back into it and spreading her fingers, tense, gripping at nothing but tile, the young woman named Jess screamed and her body shook as she gaped wide at the open maw coming straight for her, to take her whole.

Melody blanched, blinking on her hands and knees as she saw what remained of the limp body of Jess, naked, cock once dangling limply, untouched, shaven pink and resting against swollen testicles of a pubic region shaven clean, her left leg limply being inhaled. The foot shifted in the maw, still protruding before a long tongue, as pink as the shaft within, reached out, wrapping itself around the ankle, and the calf disappeared into the mouth, the beast swallowing.

There was an echoing belch and the monster, embarrassed by the sound it had just made, covered its lips, appearing tipsy as it uttered an "uh, oh" and glanced towards Melody as she stood slowly, turning her wounded gaze back at the other still standing in the locker room. Turning back, she stared towards the corner where the monster had been. Tentacles and all, having devoured the three before her eyes.

The naked form of Luna was there now, her head and body wet from the showers surrounding them all. She lowered her slim fingers to her stomach and looking

down, uncertain, she gazed back up at
Melody. Her eyes blazed.

A smile spread across her lips and
there was an echo of the slightest giggle.

# | 9

She woke with a start, in her bed once again. A dream, it seemed, as daylight streamed in the window. Filling her room. Only it was an unaware concept that filtered through her mind that seemed to warrant a question while Melody gazed upon the stereo in the corner of her closet, hearing the song.

We sing . . . *la*, LA

*"The Golden age of Grotesque."*

| *Monday*

| *Wednesday*

| Thursday & now
Friday

# | 10

Melody sat in class, her head down, her arm surrounded by the black hair she had died less than a week ago. Her body felt sore, her lap filled with the flame of a sharpening lust. She could tell she needed to jack off, but she couldn't will herself to do it. It was almost like denial, the wonder she had still on the backdraft of a memory only she seemed to understand as her own.

Was it real? Had it been?

Three people, some she had only known very quickly. Had dissolved, in a stomach contents, of an unknown realism in a nightmare she had . . . or *was* it tho?

Fake.

Shaking her head, Melody found she was annoyed. A week had passed. Only she felt she had witnessed it to be real. The fact she had seen it. Not the way anyone *else* could have but she had witnessed the agony of being kicked and somehow now felt, absolutely-

Nothing.

"Melody?"

Her face lifted from the desk and Melody stared up in a look of dazed amusement as she saw around her, the room was now empty and standing next to her, her teacher, Mrs. Eccleston was gazing upon her. Her dark brooding eyes beneath blonde brows and dirty blonde hair coifed to make a stare of realistic concern appear kind and wondering.

It was unknown the intent she seemed to have it was almost annoying. She wanted to be understanding.

Melody knew this, but ...

"You seem concerned."

"Yes," the teacher said. She glanced over her shoulder, staring at the picture of the empty room. She saw the door shut, closed. The hallway beyond noiseless but not empty. Now and then, a figure passed, but other than *that-*

"What do you want?" Melody said.

Mrs. Eccleston stared at her again, furrowing her brow. She smiled slightly, the corners of her lips appearing to be somewhat formed of a slight age. Showing what looked like closer to the early thirties.

"You need to be able to understand I'm here for you to talk to if you need someone to listen. I'm only trying to help."

Melody groaned, covering her face with her hair again.

"Join the *club*."

A moment of pause. As she turned her face slightly to peek through her hair, she saw what appeared to be-

Mrs. Eccleston?

But was it *tho?*

Seeing the features, the Asian eyes, below brazen brows of-

Black was it?

Then, Melody blinked.

# | 11

The shirt was loosened, revealing the swell of pale breast and skin, areolas pink and inflamed. A tipsy smile played on her teacher's pair of lips below the slightly small black freckle under her nose.

"Mrs. Eccleston?" Melody said.

Taking hold of her hand, she touched her student's fingers, taking hold of her fingers in her own, and stepping around the desk, crouched, as if it was to seem, at the front of class, she was kneeling down. Melody, feeling the tension between the moment of how she was understanding this, a confused and slightly wonderous gaze looking back at her from within the soul of a body and a person she had known for the rest of her senior year alone.

"Mrs. Ec-?"

SHHH*hhh*

The same whisper. The same tone of concern. Melody felt the pressure of the teacher's gaze, eying her expression of wonder, concern. Almost unethically, the realism, the dart of some unknown pleasure filled her chest with uneasiness and anxiety, followed by the burning swell between her legs. She felt the function of the erection there, slowly dwelling to be the most violent of heats causing her to feel the tenderness of the fingers between her legs as her thighs were spread open.

Shock overtook, Melody sitting back as she reached out to push her back, yet her hand froze . . . only inches from the woman's face.

The tongue licked, tenderly, almost carefully, caressing each slender tip, then, around the wrist, the lips moved, kissing pleasurably, understanding the affection the unknown flame that grew between the young woman's thighs before it. The other hand lent a quick gist of undoing the zipper and reaching in, found the pulsing throb of organ that rested, pressed hard against the tight denim. The dark eyes of Mrs. Eccleston turned upon the lap and as a sudden grin spread across her pale face. She was wearing a dark jacket underneath her shirt and she spread the fabric of her clothes to reach over and bring the hand of Melody's to her chest, touching her tit. "Feel the hardness you've given me?" she asked.

Melody gasped, feeling the tender, pale, cool fingers caressing her shaft within her jeans. As she watched the teacher pulled her out and still rubbing the swollen of her nether region, squeezed firmly to grope the glands, almost pressing the fluid growing within into the base of her balls as she gave a whimper.

"Let me show you . . . my appreciation for your, proper, conduct." Leaning forward, the other woman traced her tongue around the slender shaft, careful to tease the part just below the opening of the urethra, a g-spot, she knew, amongst other men she had held a relationship with.

Melody watched, her eyes wide with unknown lust and as her instructor's lips parted, the mouth opening, slowly, and inch by inch, inhaling her shaft, she felt the heat

within the mouth, and herself, gliding
further, deeper into the recesses of the open
throat and gullet within beyond the back of
the tongue which as the mouth closed over,
wrapped at the base of her shaft and ...
almost seemed to tease her lower testicles
which were still confined within her jeans.

"Mmm."

"Mrs. Eccleston," Melody whispered,
gazing back to the doorway which remained
closed. As she turned back she felt the lips
tightening, the suction growing complete.
Her teacher was sucking her. Sucking her off
in the middle of her classroom. The dirty
fantasies she had kept, locked away inside her
memory of imagining this before. She had
seen Mrs. Eccleston and before only once
had witnessed her bend over at the front of
class but from there, she had only seen her
midriff once and the shock of witnessing her
lips on her shaft . . .

"Mmm*hmm*."

*Oh, God.* Melody's brow knitted, in
what she couldn't tell her feelings any longer.
She gripped the back of her chair, watching

the woman's lips moved, still wrapped firmly around her cock. She felt the tightness, the taut lips moving, as Mrs. Eccleston pulled back, working her mouth as if she were drinking her.

It was so ... *dirty*.

# | 12

She felt she wouldn't last.

Staring into the bathroom mirror, Shannon gazed into the open mirrored image of herself as she saw the gaze that she was receiving back. The image of her face in ruined mascara shaded by the picture of what she could see as a reflection, almost mimicked by the fact that something else was going to happen.

Her eyes felt heavy, her body a dead weight. She gripped the rusted porcelain and then pressing her head to the faucet below, drank well-like tasting water from the spigot and smelled the aroma of her perfume flooding the air from her hair having been given the option to accept her job at the desk this week.

It had been a long one.

Shaking her head, she stepped back, and placing her fingers under eyes, saw the gaze she was witnessing back in the mirror with the reflection of knowing she wished she could quit writing this essay. This ... school page. She was trying to make such a report that it would seem almost unbelievable.

*Three.*

Shaking her head, she bit her bottom lip and Shannon walked to the fogged window glass near the wall that stretched towards the ceiling. An image of the outside blocked through the freckled glass that revealed only her shaded and screwed up image of who she was on the inside. Hanging her head, she pressed her finger against the outside glass and felt the chill of the coming winter. She could see the way the ground was going to freeze; she saw the change of the autumn in the trees. The only thing she didn't believe was what she had witnessed.

Three popular girls, she thought. One new. One part of a group of three older seniors that had echoed a painless witness to a quick yet . . . was it an attractive demise.

She didn't know if she could trust herself to believe she was seeing herself to believe this was real.

Biting her bottom lip, she dragged herself to the wall and slumped down, seeing the tiled floor at her feet and slumping down, she slid over the wall to sit down, resting her right leg across the floor and then absentmindedly throwing up her right hand to her forehead, pressed her fingers against her forehead and then rubbed her left eye, raising her knees to her chest and hugging them to her chest. She remained uncertain.

She didn't know who to trust. Was it right of her to write this essay. A paper about something that no one would ever seem to remember except maybe her? Was she to believe it right? Was it safe? Was she going to see the end of her senior year or end up-?

She let the question leave as she recalled the stare. The look of fear in the other girl, the last one to see herself be eaten. Bess was her name? Cass? She didn't remember. Sleep had left her destabilized by the echo of what she had witnessed. The look of panic before the last blink of an eye and only a dangling leg had been hanging from the open mouth, just as the long tongue wrapped around and swallowed the young woman whole.

*Then.*

She unfurled her legs, letting them slide out in front of her. She yawned, putting a hand over her mouth to stifle sleep. Another question had come to her mind. Her memory fogged. She scratched her ear behind the lobe of her left piercing and remained certain she couldn't remember what the name was.

Something like a moon? Loon. *Moon?*

Then, it came, fast and quick, almost like a snap of fingers in her face. She remembered the caramel skin, almost pale under the water dripping from her hair. The way her stomach was taut, her breasts full yet tight against her flat ribcage which showed no sign of having consumed. The image of her smile and the way she had looked down, touching her stomach, looking at *her* . . .

The other woman. The other senior. Who was *she?*

Biting her bottom lip, Shannon yawned once more, and struggled to cope with her sudden fear. All at once she had a feeling ... a reason to be connected. To know the pipeline within her school. She found herself struggling to compare her options and find out why she was so scared; was there anyone, someone whom she'd be able to trust? Anyone she could talk to.

Her thoughts left a moment, as she listened to what sounded like rustling in the trees, the branches beyond the glass. Dead leaves were falling, followed by the sound of distant thunder in the fall. The noise of a coming storm.

The young woman. The other girl in the room who had not been swallowed, yet had witnessed the feast of bullies, second to last, the one who had kicked her low, forced her to perform cunnilingus.

Her mouth watered. Shannon felt her heart hammering in her chest, quickly, sudden. Anxiety and panic filled her body and she did not understand why. Her eyes drifted across the rest room, the stalls lining the wall, the open void of each leading to a release of the bowels within her yet she didn't have to use the bathroom. She was here, consulting with herself.

Understanding . . . *Why?*

Lifting herself from the floor, she stood up, looking at the stalls, feeling her stomach, twisting, churning suddenly as she stumbled towards one of the open jon, and as she pushed open the door, she found her moment of fear dissipate, if only for a moment as she stumbled in, forward pitch, and sunk to her knees before throne. Her insides heaved, and her body trembled, shaking from the stress of emptying almost nothing from last night. Sour, black bile filled the bowl and she found her eyes watering from the agony of having an empty chest. She retched again, and as she found her body twisting in vain from the strain of collab with her sharpening thoughts and wit that was . . . not to be... she couldn't almost hear the noise. A sound that was both unnerving and it made her ears perk up despite being so tired. She suddenly felt more awake.

Resting back, within the door frame, and beyond the crack of the frame from the tile below and into the shadows near the jon, Shannon felt her heart still beating, the creak of the seat beside her, the sour bile filled porcelain, the wet stink of her stomach now floating, soon to fill the storm drains below. She reached up, hesitant, before flushing the remains, hearing the drain gurgling below and almost feeling the hum of her stomach contents returning to the below, where the gravel remained to be whole again, only if years before the maker called her soul to the home above.

But *below*.

The sound of the creaking could be heard, only once more, her ears filling with the sound of the echo, a non, but still chilling sound that seemed almost uncommonly terrifying as her chest seemed to convulse most fluently with the dream that, somehow, she was in a void. A different place, knowing how tired she had been, the afternoon before.

*Her secret.*

Her secret was *coming ...*

Shannon thought about the paper. She thought about the realism of her story, knowing how almost unplanned, how uncertain it would seem that she, she herself was one of the few in the school where everyone had been going, where everyone had been attending the realistic station where learning could be an option, for many. Those who were friends; those popular; those who were realistically framing themselves to be-

-swallo*wed.*

A bump, and the slightest turn of her face and it seemed-

No, it *couldn't-*

Be *real.*

Shannon gazed, almost in fear at the darkness of the face, the features that seemed somehow enormous, the glare of such an enormous eye, with in the face of something she felt was unreal.

I must be dreaming, she thought to herself. She saw the figure materialized, somehow still unseen, though just how enormous the face appeared, and she saw the fingers, rising out, and above to show the signs that there was almost a dark share of the smoke she could inhale, like an essence of sharp distant and twisting vapors that were like some *sort* of . . .

Sharply, the grasping fingers curled around her body, dragging her across the floor and up, her body feeling heavy, yet lighter than air as she was raised to the smiling, grinning teeth that bared a deeper void beyond the grin where she could see the image of what was beyond the realm of the jon, and up into the glare of yellow beams that shone like ethereal headlights, almost unshared by the mystics of a worst nightmare. Her panic rose slightly as the fingers seemed to reach around from the second hand and she found herself floating.

She closed her eyes.

# | 13

She knew she wasn't going to last long.

Melody bit her lower lip, facing the imagery of sudden imaginary fate within the face before her. The woman smiled her lips filled with the meat of her trans women hood. She could feel her cock pulsating within the warm mouth, as if abandoning all hope to remain silent and she knew she was going to burst, as if soon the feeling would erupt and her soul would be lost.

"Mrs. Eccleston," she gasped, her legs trembling, "I'm going to, I'm gonna-"

"Mmhm."

Her voice grew strained, the orgasm coming so intensely she could feel her body gearing up for an intense sensation, the moment almost nearing so quick she could feel her member gaining the explosion like a sudden rocket of amazement and claim that she knew was only a dream of hers sometime before. But now was a reality.

"Mrs. Eccleston! UHHHGGGGNNNNN!"

Cum. Jets of it, flooded the throat as her cock trembled, the twitching organ releasing the dream cream she had held on for so long, knowing the solution to only one was that she use her own fingers to salivate upon and imagine the reality to be a fake dream in itself.

But now it was real. Now it was a sudden imaginary factoid that had come to life. She could not, deny herself the understanding that this was actually happening.

"Oh, *fuck*." Melody gasped, her thighs trembling before gazing down at the woman in her lap. Her eyes gazed upon the dark brows and the brown eyes below, seeing the image of what appeared as Mrs. Eccleston.

But it wasn't.

"Luna?"

# | 13

She stood, alone, naked, in her backyard, suddenly enveloped by the downpour of rain from the grey sky above. It seemed so dim outside, the overcast of clouds above echoing the lightning stretching across the sky. Melody gazed up, her hair wet as she saw the face and features of a person she felt she knew, and in image a force of some sort of imaginary fate wrinkled with time almost seemingly filled with hatred now as the hand came down, scooping her up into his fingers, curling around her body, and pulling her up towards the grinning mouth.

Melody felt herself in panic, as if struggling to understand the dilemma. She watched the lips moving, as if in fate of her knowing already the jig was up. She saw the eyes roving to see her and as the palm lifted, the fingers opening to touch the shaft between her legs as it twitched in thought of the largeness, the openness within, the tongue snaked out from between the lips and licked the tip, teasing almost before the mouth opened and gapingly so, engulfed her member in the intense heat of what was to be her mouth.

The tongue was the muscle that worked, teasing her to beyond the imaginary thought of her reality. Almost drunkenly and somewhat feeble, Melody tried to push herself away. She couldn't, and her eyes took in the mouth as it worked, a stronger suction than any she had ever known.

"Oh, uhgn, *fuck*."

So close. She was getting so close. Closer and closer still to the edge and she knew that Luna knew. She saw her face as she was gazing upon her expression of shocked ecstasy and betrayal.

Suddenly, she was lifted, high into the air and as the mouth gaped again, her body writhed before the maw came closer and she disappeared into the parted lips.

Luna savored the wriggling fear within the body, the tension of a soul that she now possessed to her gullet and tasting the drip of still unwilling precum at the tip of the cock, she lifted her head back and opening her throat, inhaled the body of Melody who disappeared into her stomach from the esophagus. A slight aftertaste of spunk followed, somewhat sweet, yet salty.

"Mm," she said. "Mm, *hm*."

The eyes of Luna turned red. Then, as the succubus grinned, she turned around and faced the neighborhood before gazing up and into the shock of the next flash of lighting she was gone.

Melody was no more.

Made in the USA
Columbia, SC
22 July 2024

39174529R00037